To all my Cronulla mermaids. *R.C.*

Love & splashes for Finola. *A.J.*

Chapter One

Crystal had been a fairy once. But that was when she was only three. Now that she was older, she knew what she was going to be. A mermaid!

1

She did everything she could think of to make it happen. She swung her legs under her chair while she had breakfast. Then she walked with tiny little steps when she got down from the table.

'I'm a mermaid,' she said to Mum and Dad.

'Well, you've got the right hair for it,' said Mum.

Dad had once said her

hair reminded him of
seaweed. Now she didn't
mind that at all!

At the beach she swam
with her ankles together.

Until her ankle bones got
too sore. Then she sat on
a rock and combed her hair.
She used the comb Mum
kept in her swimming bag.

It was old and yellow and it looked a bit like fish bones.

Crystal held her breath in the bath to see how long she could stay under.

'Don't do that,' said Dad.

She even tried to fit both legs into one side of her green pyjama pants, and every night, before she went to sleep, she made a very special wish.

'I wish I was a mermaid,'

she said with her eyes shut
very tight.

But no matter how many
things Crystal tried,
nothing she did ever
seemed to work.

'What do I have to do
to be a mermaid, Mum?'
she asked one night.

Mum helped her put her
pyjamas on the right way.
Then she gave her a kiss
and tucked her in.

'You leave that to me,'
said Mum.

Chapter Two

Mum made clothes for a
stall she had at the Sunday
markets.

She made crumpled skirts
that opened up like fans.
She made puffy pants that

filled up like balloons. They
had rainbow colours, and
tinkling bells, and stars,
and moons, and feathers.

Crystal loved the things
Mum made.

'Wake up, Crystal,' Dad
called out on Sunday
morning. 'Mum's got a
surprise for you.'

She ran into Mum and
Dad's room and climbed into
the big bed.

'Mum's been up half the
night,' said Dad.

Mum yawned and took something out of her sewing bag. She stretched it around Crystal's waist and said, 'I hope it fits.'

Crystal was so happy she  couldn't think of what to say. While she had been asleep last night Mum had made a mermaid tail.

Chapter Three

She pulled the tail on.
It was nice and tight and
there was a hole at the
bottom for her feet. It was
covered all over with deep
green and blue sequins.

'Come on,' said Mum.

'You can leave it on to go to the markets.'

Crystal swung her tail under her stool while she had breakfast. It flashed and sparkled in the morning sun. Then she walked with tiny little steps, up and down the

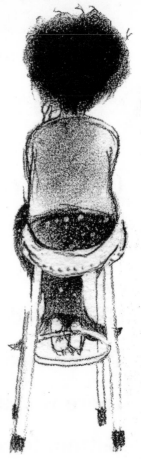

rows of stalls. The other stall holders all watched and smiled.

When the markets closed, they packed up and went home. Crystal sat in the front of the van. Dad parked outside their flat and ran upstairs for his surfboard.

'Time to hit the beach!' he said, when he came back.

Crystal played in
the sand in the
afternoon while her
mother made her
a seashell top.

'What do you think
of that?' said Mum.

They sat together
on a rock to watch
Dad surf.

Then, when it
was nearly dark, Dad
carried her home and ran

a bath. It was almost as
if Mum and Dad had

found her washed up
on the shore.

'Can I wear my tail
in the bath?' she asked.
She had her fingers crossed
behind her back.

'I guess it would be all
right,' said Dad.

Crystal splashed and
splashed. Water went
everywhere. She let
her hair float all around
her head. She squirted

water spouts as high as
she could.

She didn't want to get
out of the bath at all. Not
even when the water got
cold. But Mum said she
had to get
ready for
bed.

She had
prunes on
her fingers
when Dad
lifted her
out.

'Would I turn into a real mermaid if I wore my tail to bed?' she asked.

'I'm afraid it's a bit wet for that,' said Dad.

Chapter Four

On Monday morning Mum
said she could take her
mermaid tail to school.

Crystal showed all her
friends at break. She could
tell they wished they had

tails as well. Mrs Winton,

her teacher, said she was

the first mermaid they'd had

at Shelly Beach Primary.

Then Mum and Dad
picked her up after school.
'It's so hot,' said Mum.
'I thought we could go to
the pool!'

Crystal's heart jumped.
She imagined the lifeguard
finding a mermaid
swimming around in the
deep end.

When they got to the
pool she quickly ran to get
changed. She didn't want
anyone seeing her without
her tail.

She wobbled out of the
changing room when she
was ready.

Crystal stood on
the edge of the pool. She
took a big breath. She
looked around at the other
kids.

'Come on, Mermaid, jump!' said Dad, and Crystal did.

Then a moment later she popped out of the water like a cork!

The tail made her feel very brave. She jumped into Dad's arms again and again.

But somehow she couldn't open her eyes under the water.

She stayed in a lot longer than she ever had. She tried doing forward rolls and backward flips. But she couldn't hold her breath for very long either.

After a while she began to feel cold. She made two fists and rubbed her eyes.

'Come on,' said Dad.

'Time to get out.'

'But a real mermaid
wouldn't get out yet.' Crystal
almost cried.

'What's the matter?' asked
Mum.

'It still isn't like being a
real mermaid,' said Crystal.

Chapter Five

Crystal hoped that if she wore her tail long enough something magic might happen.

At school she wore it for break and lunch.

At home she wore it every
night in the bath.

She even wore it on Friday
night to go late-night shopping.

Crystal walked with tiny
little steps all around the
supermarket. But her
mermaid tail kept falling
down.

'Come on,' said Dad.
'Do you want a ride?'

She swung her tail onto
the shopping trolley. But the
blue and green sequins kept
dropping off.

'At least we will find our way
home again,' Dad laughed.

It was too late for a bath by the time they got home.

'Straight to bed for you,' said Dad.

Crystal wriggled carefully out of her mermaid tail and hung it on the back of her bedroom door. Another blue sequin fell to the floor. It made her sad.

'Night, night,' said Dad. 'Sweet dreams.'

She curled her legs up

in the dark and stared out the window at the stars.

She still hadn't worn her tail to bed. Somehow it had always been too wet. But it wasn't tonight.

She didn't think Mum and Dad would mind if she wore it just this once . . .

Chapter Six

'Ee, ee, ee, ee.' Crystal heard a strange sound. She opened her eyes and looked around.

A real, live dolphin was tapping at her bedroom window!

She looked at the floor.
It was covered with sand!
Seaweed was growing
out from under her bed!
A tiny crab was hiding
in the corner under her
dresser!

Crystal pulled back her
quilt and looked at her tail.
It was smooth, and wet,
and scaly.

She gave her tail a
flick. It didn't fall down.

It flashed and sparkled as
if it were made of silver.

Crystal did a forward roll
with joy. The dolphin did
one at the window.

Just for fun she did
a backward flip as well.
So did the dolphin!

Crystal opened the
window and swam out into
the ocean. Then she and
the dolphin swam all the
way to the top.

Whoosh! They both leapt as high as they could out of the water.

When they came back down they made an enormous splash. The dolphin clapped his flippers together and made Crystal laugh.

She loved being a mermaid. It was like having a clown for your birthday party. Only better.

Crystal flicked her flashing silver tail. She thought she could stay a mermaid forever and ever.

Chapter Seven

Crystal did all the things
she used to imagine herself
doing.

She flopped her tail
around lazily while she had
breakfast. (She ate raw

oysters straight out of their
shells!)

Then she wriggled her
tail as fast as she could
when she and the dolphin
went for a swim.

'I'm a mermaid!' she said
to herself.

The dolphin just nodded
his head and laughed. It
was almost as if he knew
what she was thinking.

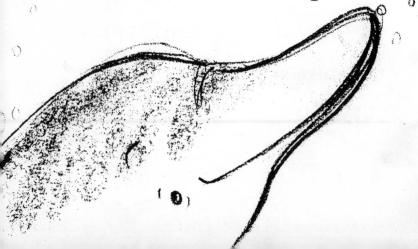

On the bottom of the
ocean they played in a
garden of kelp. It swished
and rolled in the current.

Then they tickled giant
clams with the tips of their
tails.

Crystal squealed when they made them snap their shells closed.

They threw coloured starfish back and forth to each other as if they were frisbees.

'Ee, ee, ee, ee,' the dolphin said, balancing an orange starfish on his head.

Crystal collected more and more to see how many he could balance.

Then they flicked their
tails and swam
away.

Crystal and the dolphin spent the whole day playing under the ocean.

They scattered schools of glistening fish and flipped giant jellyfish over.

But then, at last, Crystal began to feel tired. She found herself thinking about Mum and Dad and suddenly she knew she would miss them too much

if she stayed a mermaid
forever.

The dolphin swam over
and gently nuzzled into her
shoulder.

'Ee, ee, ee, ee,' the
dolphin said, and somehow
Crystal understood what
he meant.

She looked up and saw
the bottom of Dad's
surfboard floating on the
surface.

Crystal smiled and said
goodbye to the dolphin.

Up, and up, and up she
swam.

'Hello, little mermaid,'

said Dad.

Chapter Eight

'Hello, little mermaid,' said
Dad. 'What's happened to
your tail?'

Crystal's mermaid tail
was on the floor.

Dad hung it up on the

back of the door. 'I think your tail's seen better days,' said Dad.

'Oh well,' said Crystal. 'I don't really mind.'

She ran into Mum and Dad's room and climbed into the big bed.

Crystal yawned and
stretched her arms up high.

'Mum,' she said.

'Hmm?' said Mum.

'I want to be a butterfly,' said Crystal.

From Raewyn Caisley

When I was young I longed to be a mermaid and, even now, when I'm diving beneath the waves, it still sounds like a nice idea.

I wrote this story while I was sitting on Cronulla Beach. Lots of mermaids came to help.

From Ann James

I loved illustrating this story because, just like Crystal, I have a fascination with mermaids. When I was a little girl I knew a mermaid. Her name was Anemone. I met her first when I was sitting on a rock looking into the rock pool. She looked exactly like me, except, you know what? She had a tail like a fish.

Over the years I've learnt to swim strongly and can hold my breath for a very long time.

Look out for these other
Happy Cat First Readers.

No one believes in unicorns any more. Except Princess Lily, that is.
So when the king falls ill and the only thing that can cure him is
the magic of a unicorn, it's up to her to find one.
But can Lily find a magical unicorn in time?

Nicholas Nosh is the littlest pirate in the world. He's not allowed to go to sea. 'You're too small,' said his dad. But when the fierce pirate Captain Red Beard kidnaps his family, Nicholas sets sail to rescue them!

Nobody is better at being bad than Buster Reed – he flicks
paint, says rude words to girls, sticks chewing gum under
the seats and wears the same socks for weeks at a time.
Naturally no one wants to know him. But Buster has a
secret – he would like a friend to play with.
How will he ever manage to find one?

When Anna
Slept Over

Jane Godwin

Josie is Anna's best friend. Anna has played at Josie's house,
she's even stayed for dinner, but she has never slept over.
Until now…

The Magic Wand

Ursula Dubosarsky

Becky was cross with her little brother. 'If you don't leave me alone,' she said to him, 'I'll put a spell on you!' But she didn't mean to make him disappear!

The Gorilla Suit

Victor Kelleher

Tom was given a gorilla suit for his birthday. He loved it and wore
it everywhere. When mum and dad took him to the zoo he
wouldn't wear his ordinary clothes. But isn't it asking for trouble
to go to the zoo dressed as a gorilla?

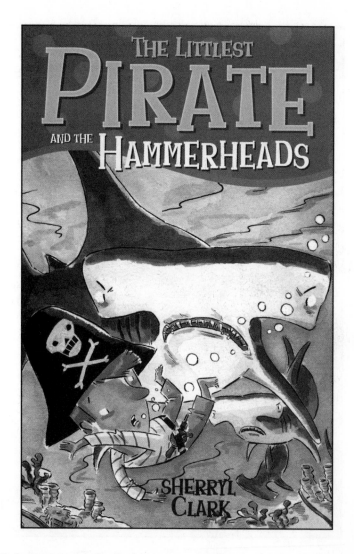

Nicholas Nosh, the littlest pirate in the world, has to rescue his family's treasure which has been stolen by Captain Hammerhead. But how can he outwit the sharks that are guarding Captain Hammerhead's ship?

Other Happy Cat books you might enjoy.

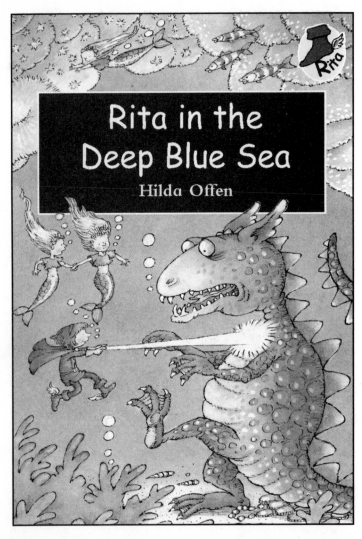

Rita in the Deep Blue Sea

Hilda Offen

Rita's mother won't let her go on a boat with her brothers and sister. However, when she has changed into her Rescuer outfit she can ride on a turtle, tie an octopus in knots and even get the better of a mermaid-eating sea-monster!

Septimouse is the seventh son of a seventh son which makes him a truly magical mouse. Septimouse can talk to cats and humans too – he can even make them as tiny as he is. But the one thing he can't seem to do is to get his paws on some cheese!

The supermouse has won the Cheese of the Year competition and
now longs for fame and fortune. If only his prize-winning cheese
recipe didn't have to be kept secret! Then disaster strikes –
only Septimouse can save the day!